to Floosie
who is very silly

Babette Cole
The Silly Book

Doubleday
New York London Toronto Sydney Auckland

If you look closely you'll agree,
there are some silly sights to see.

Silly people passing by
have silly walks
that you can try!

Silly ears

and silly necks,

silly noses,

silly specs.

Silly beards

and silly teeth,

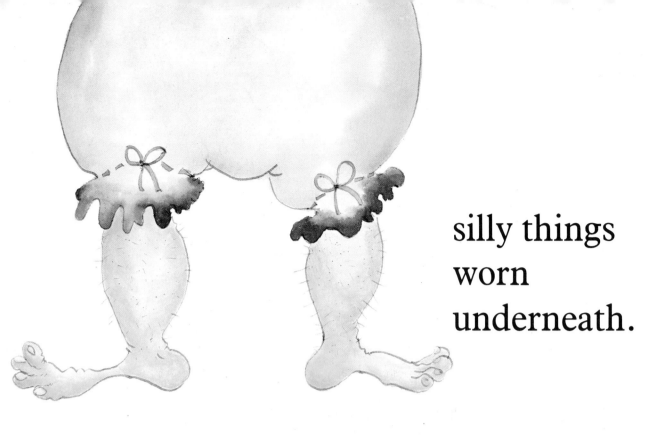

silly things
worn
underneath.

Silly hats are there to hide
some very silly heads
inside!

And have you seen
how odd it gets

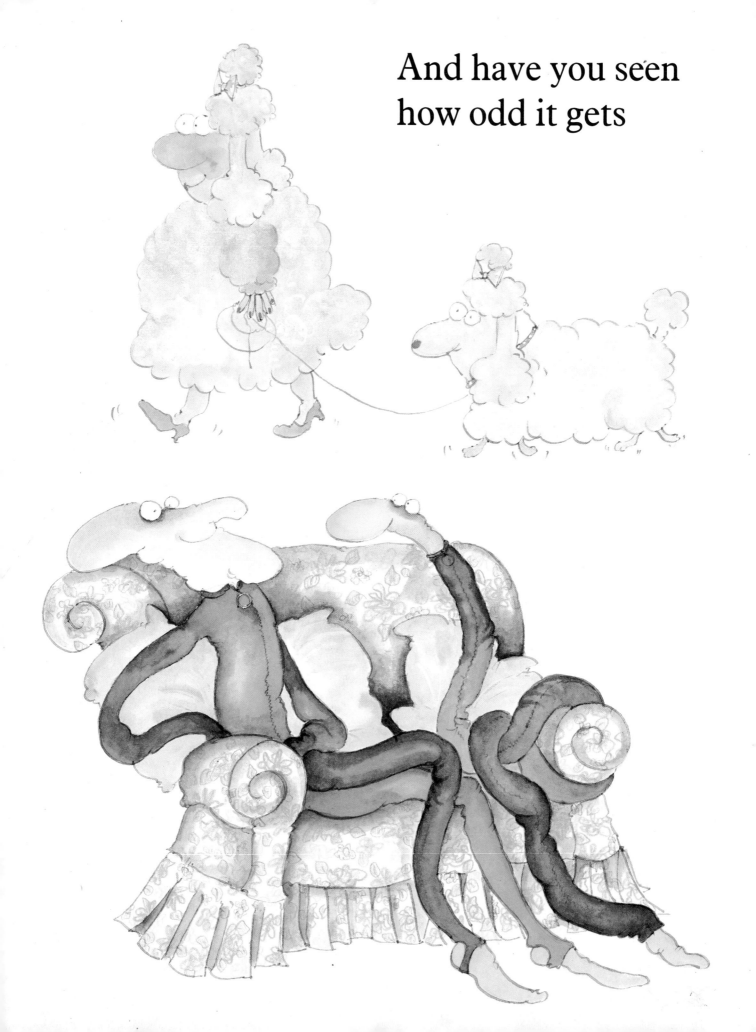

when silly folks
look like their pets?

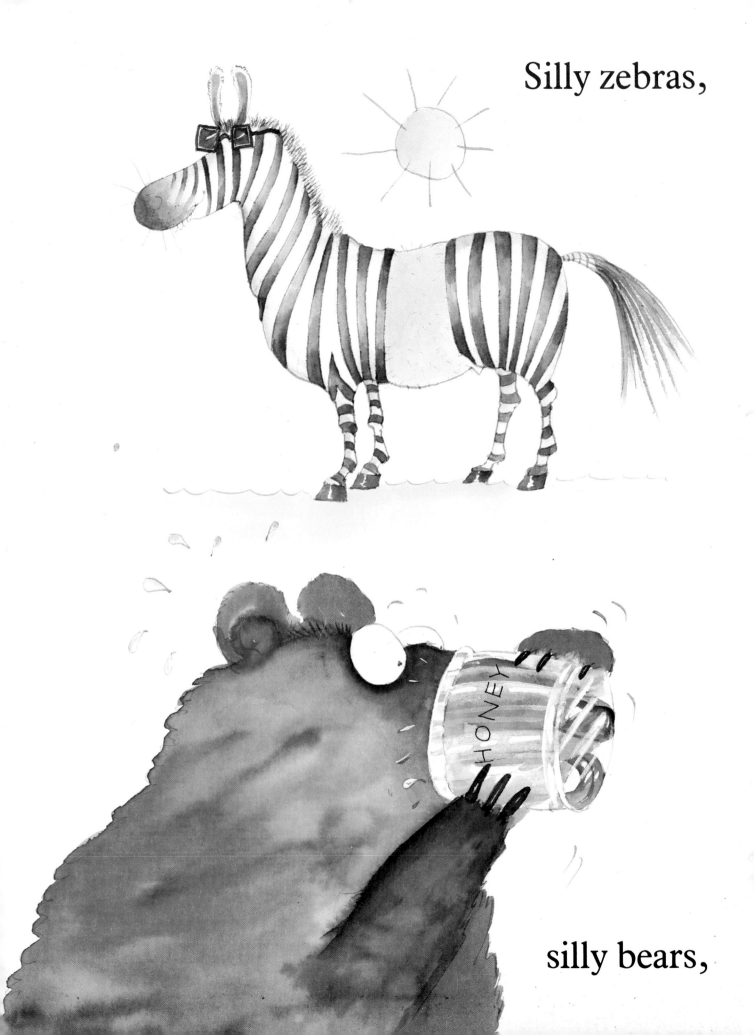

Silly zebras,

silly bears,

silly sharks

and silly hares.

My best friend, silly Ernie Klapp,
built himself a big mole trap.
The moles had made a bigger kind
and quickly caught him from behind.

Some silly people like to fly,

I've never known
the reason why.

Babies eat some silly things,
like flies with wriggly legs and wings.

But grown-ups enjoy silly feasts
of snails and frogs

and wriggly beasts

My uncle Billy ate some fire.

His temperature went higher and higher!

But auntie got the teapot spout and put poor silly Billy out!

His friend, the Nabob of Namphilly,
had forty wives and all were silly.

They tickled him and not one stopped
until the poor old Nabob popped!

So don't play

silly party tricks

and scare
your friends

out of their wits . . .

With silly masks

and silly sheets,

for they can cause some silly SHRIEKS!

I hate being dressed in silly best,

with collar and
cuffs all frilly.

I'd rather
wear my
plain wool suit . . .

I don't think
it's silly

Published by Doubleday,
a division of Bantam Doubleday Dell Publishing Group, Inc.
666 Fifth Avenue, New York, New York 10103

Doubleday and the portrayal of an anchor
with a dolphin are trademarks of Doubleday,
a division of Bantam Doubleday Dell Publishing Group, Inc.

Library of Congress Catalog Card Number 89-37380

ISBN 0-385-41237-1
ISBN 0-385-41238-X (lib. bdg.)

Copyright © 1989 by Babette Cole
First published in 1989 by Jonathan Cape Ltd, 32 Bedford Square, London WC1B 3SG.